Anonymous

Life's Comedy

Anonymous

Life's Comedy

ISBN/EAN: 9783337104023

Printed in Europe, USA, Canada, Australia, Japan

Cover: Foto ©Andreas Hilbeck / pixelio.de

More available books at **www.hansebooks.com**

LIFE'S COMEDY

THIRD · SERIES

CHARLES SCRIBNER'S SONS

LIFE'S COMEDY

THIRD SERIES

CHARLES SCRIBNER'S SONS
NEW YORK, MDCCCXCVIII

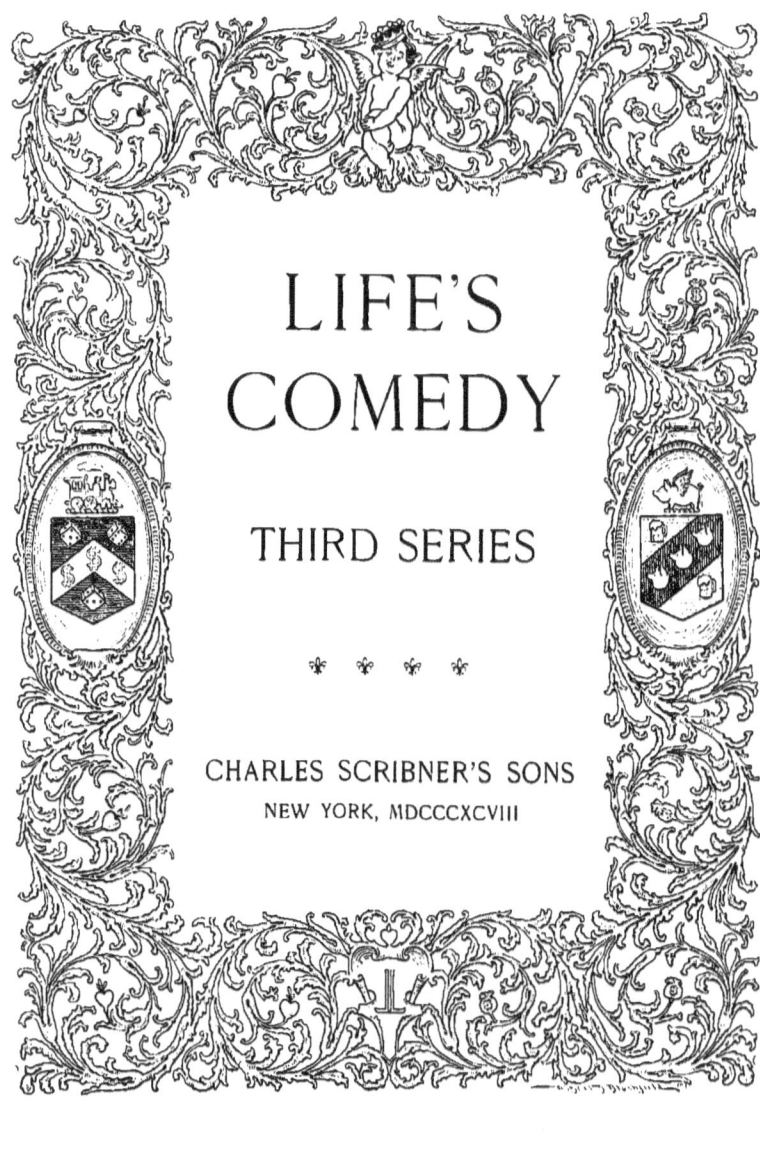

LIST OF ARTISTS.

LOVE AND FOLLY.

MAIDS, WIVES AND WIDOWS.

LORDS OF CREATION.

ALL SORTS AND CONDITIONS.

LIFE'S COMEDY.

LOVE AND FOLLY.

"Is he really so dissipated?"

"Oh, no; that's emotion. Last night when he called on me I felt his arm shake."

LOVE AND FOLLY.

ALL ABOARD!
JUST two minutes more.
O Tempus, stand still!
Stand still, I implore,
One moment until
I have time to reflect
On what I would say;
Give me time to collect
My senses, I pray,
Until I have said
What my courage was mounting
To say—when, instead,
I was stupidly counting
The moments that fled.
O Tempus, you're flying!
A plague on this parting—
This flying, good-bying—
This smiling and smarting;
A plague, too, upon
This—heavens, it's starting!
All aboard!—
There, she's gone.
Oliver Herford
O Herford

"I am engaged to marry Miss Hungerford, dad."
"Can she support a husband?"

FOR ECONOMICAL REASONS

"Now that Gadkins and his wife have separated, he gives her all his income."

"Why did they separate?"

"He wanted to cut down his expenses."

WHEN POLLY WAS MY SWEET-HEART.

WHEN Polly was my sweetheart
The days went dancing by
As lightly as her laughter,
Her mocking, or her sigh;
She brought the sunshine with her,
A dawn of new delight,
And left me when we parted
To dream of her all night.

When Polly was my sweetheart
I knew no sordid care;
What gold could keep its lustre
Beside her glinting hair
And who was I, to envy
The proudest of the land,
That felt but lately on me
The touch of her dear hand!

When Polly was my sweetheart
And vowed she loved me true
I had not guessed the lurking
Of guile in eyes so blue;
Or that a cheek can offer
The same delicious rose
To greet a wooer's coming,
And speed him when he goes.

When Polly was my sweetheart
Oh, idle time and blind!
Its memories blow backward
With every April wind
Until, if I could suffer
The joy and pain of yore,
I should not mind her making
A fool of me once more. *M. E. W.*

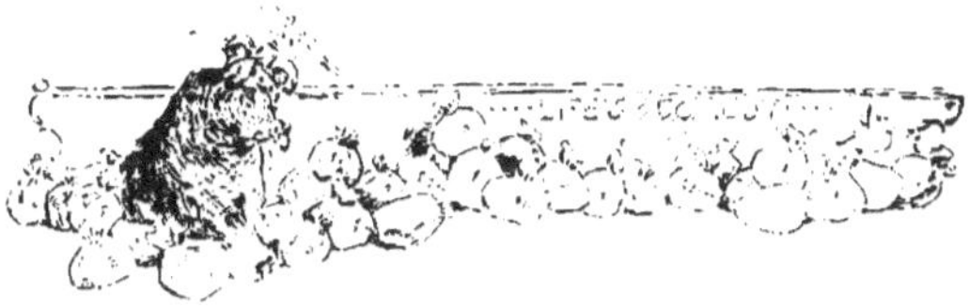

"I need the money, as I am about to be married."
"What security can you give?"
"The girl's name."

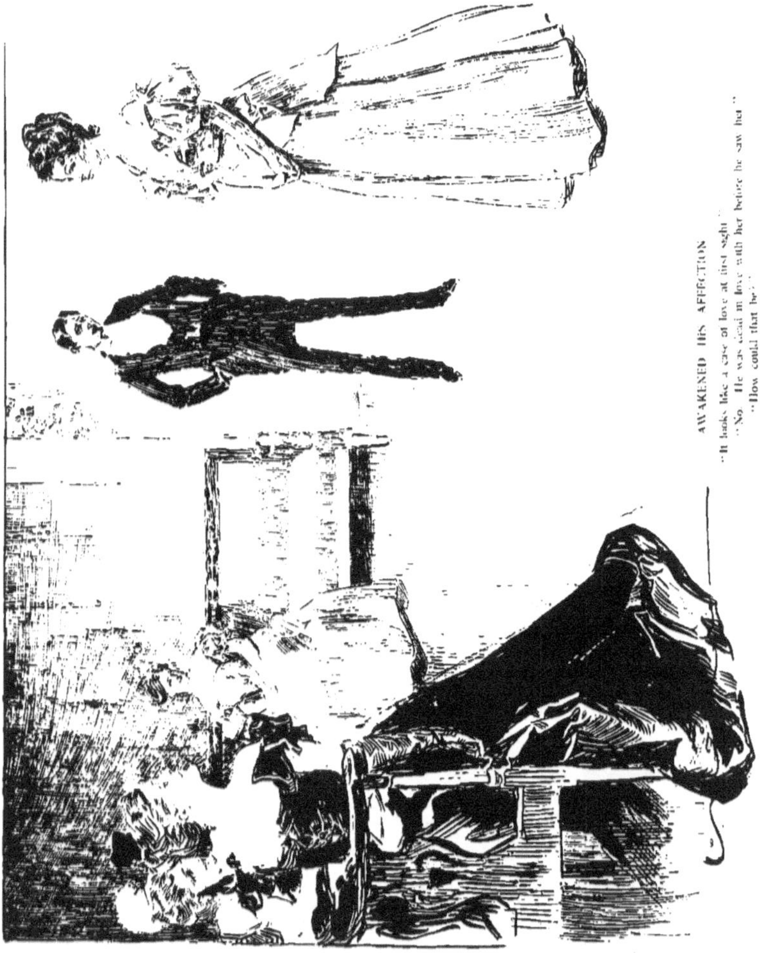

AWAKENED HIS AFFECTION.

"It looks like a case of love at first sight."

"No. He was dead in love with her before he saw her."

"How could that be?"

"$500,000 in her own right."

SHE (anxiously). Do you think, dear, that papa will consent?
"He can't help it. If he doesn't, I am going to tell him I shall leave his employ."

EVOLUTION

IN times of bluff King Hal the lads
Were wont to sue the lassies, O!
And for the fickle fair their blades
Did many thrusts and passes, O!

Cholly: The bwute! He said he would blow my brains out.
"And did he?"

But nowadays the merry fays
  Need no such hard pursuing, O!
They "catch" the *man*, and sometimes can
  Do *very* pretty wooing, O!

Otho Cushing.

A WASTED EFFORT.

She (encouragingly): It is so unjust to accuse a man of weakness because he is in love.
"Of course He may never intend to marry the woman."

THE SELF-DENYING GIRLS' RETURN TO EARTH.

THE HEART'S TRIBUNAL

THE heart her own tribunal hath
  When love is captive at the bar
However wayward be his path
  However soiled his pinions are.

Just so he sinneth not toward her,
  Though there be none to take his
    part
And witness swear, and court demur:
  "Not guilty" finds the heart!

Martha Gilbert Dickinson

A MYSTERY.

"While Miss Fitz was away George took [illegible]
"Anything happen?"
"I don't know; [illegible] and the engagement is off."

WI

LIFE'S COMEDY

AUNT: There is your favorite, Mr. Cobalt, who painted my portrait. I'm sure one would never imagine him a man of so much ability.
"And still, dear aunt, he seems a man who would not falter at any *buy* undertaking."

NOT ENOUGH.

THEY say she is a poem—
  Quite likely that may be;
I find unto my sorrow
  She is averse to me.

McLandburgh Wilson.

"You can hardly blame Fanny for marrying you for money, when you haven't a cent of your own."
"Yes, but if only one of us had done it, it wouldn't be so bad. We were *both* fooled."

NO DOUBT.

CYNTHIA (who tries to live elegantly in New York on $2,000 a year): Poor old John Miner, all his property gone, and dying in a hospital!

"Calm yourself, Cynthia. The chances are old John is dying a lot more comfortably than we are living."

DELAYS ARE DANGEROUS

"Now, my dear, you ought to go right into housekeeping as soon as you are married."
"That is the best time to begin, I suppose, while I am sure of George's love?"

1st Acquaintance: I suppose her family is of a very long descent?
2nd: I don't know—but it must be of a pretty steep descent

MYRTILLA smiles too sweet on wealthy me,
  And honeyed Chloris fills one with regret:
Swift-scornful Phyllis buzzes like a bee,
  And handsome Sappho is an arch coquette.

My fortune, heart, and big ancestral tree,
  Shall not by these be carved and made to fall;
But one apart my valentine shall be—
  Dear Laura, asking nothing, takes it all.

O. T.

"Why on earth did you bring your prayer-book to the burlesque?"
"I always carry it in my hand during Lent."

THE UNCERTAIN FUTURE

He — My darling, I always feel like taking off my shoes when I enter your sacred presence.
"Well, I would rather you did it now than after we are married."

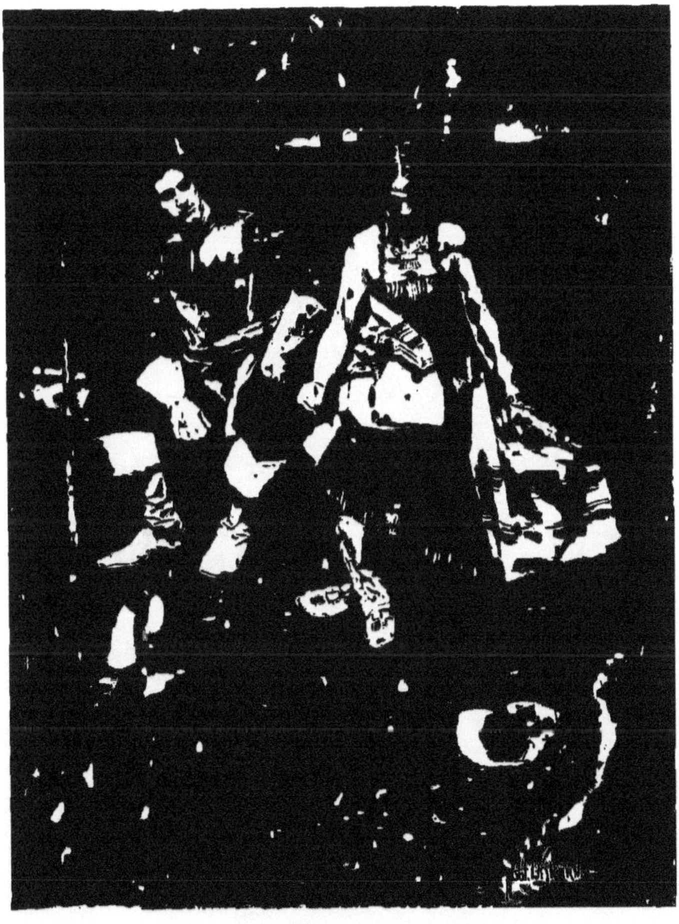

IN THE GOOD OLD DAYS

"But papa will never give his consent."

"Oh, never mind; I'll shoot papa to-morrow."

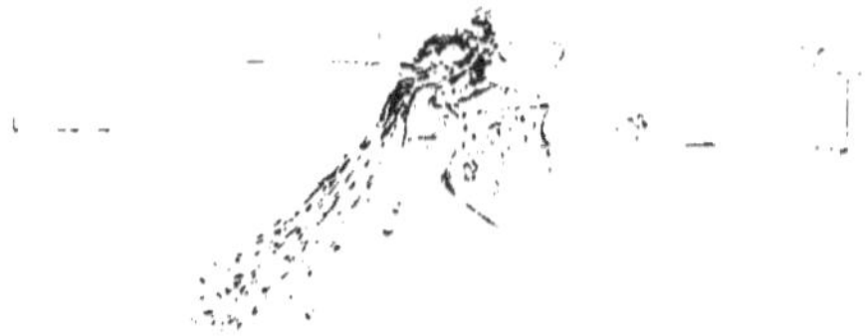

BUSINESS.

"Poor thing! Your marriage is not a success, is it?"

PROFESSIONAL BEAUTY: Oh, I don't know. I receive all the alimony I claimed.

He: When I married you, you hadn't a cent.
"Oh, yes, I had. My face was my fortune."
"Now I know what they mean when they say money talks.

MATRIMONIAL QUERY
Which?

CONJUGAL REPARTEE

"Jack, dear, it isn't a bit nice of you to let such small troubles worry you so soon after our marriage."
"They do seem insignificant when I think of that."

LOVE AND FOLLY.

A DESERT SPOON.

BEHIND THE SCENES

"How well your wife makes love!"
"She practices at home on me."

ONE MORE PROOF.

He—What will the world say at our divorce?

[illegible]—That a fool and his money are soon parted.

LIFE'S COMEDY.

MAIDS, WIVES AND WIDOWS.

SHE: There's Mrs. Smith, and her uncle was only buried yesterday
"There is only one death in her family that would keep that woman at home."
"Whose?"
"Her own."

She: Before we were married you used to say I was an angel.

"Dad used to tell me there were three celebrated liars in our town; that my brother was one, and I the other two."

"APRIL SHOWERS BRING MAY FLOWERS."

LIFE'S COMEDY.

"I fear, doctor, I am not good enough to go to church."

"But, my dear madame, it isn't your goodness, it's your desire."

"But I'm not good enough to have any desire."

READY FOR THE ROAD.

"What sort of a traveling dress did the bride wear?"
"Knickerbockers and a sweater."

·AURELIA·

HEDGED with resolutions pious,
Far away though she be nigh us,
Moves the maid demure.
Does the ægis of devotion
From all temporal emotion
Keep her thoughts secure?

Forty days, serene, unruffled,
Ears to worldly sounds close-muffled,
Time passed as a dream;
Dream, perchance of pure deeds votive,
Or were raiment fine its motive!
Good or goods its theme?

Then the chrysalis outgrowing,
To a life with splendor glowing
She again is born.
Never knows maid greater glory,
Be she in life, song or story,
Than on Easter morn.

Wood Levette Wilson.

"The way girls carry on nowadays is positively awful. The very idea of getting engaged to half a dozen men in a season! People didn't do that when I was young."

"Don't you think times have improved wonderfully since then, grandma?"

"He declares he will win me, if it takes forever. I suppose he thinks the time will come when I am so old I will *have* to take him."
"Yes, he says he will have you in another six months.

WHEN Ruby sings the songs of praise,
I quite forget my worldly ways,
And only list angelic lays,
Her voice soars high and higher;
It seems that e'en the minister
In glances gives his love to her,
Nor text to him doth e'er recur,
When Ruby's in the choir.

Her prayerful pleadings seem to rise,
Appealing both to weak and wise,
Until they reach the vaulted skies
And join with angel lyre;
And yet I fear the songs that roll
In tuneful rhyme to Heaven's goal
Beseech the heart instead of soul
When Ruby's in the choir.

Roy Farrell Greene.

"Is it any fun getting a man to teach you how to ride the wheel?"
"Fun! why, I've been taught three times."

TURNED BOTH WAYS

"That young simpleton to whom I was engaged last summer turned up yesterday."
"Gracious! You poor thing! What did you do?"
"I accepted him."

WITH CARE.

THE MOTHER. You don't mean to say, my dear, that you permitted yourself to sit on his lap?
THE DAUGHTER: Don't be alarmed, mamma. I rested partly on my toes.

TURN ABOUT IS FAIR PLAY.

Dedicated to certain ladies who are fond of wearing borrowed plumage.

A Gown of Old Brocade

SHE wore her grandma's old brocade
All trimmed with olden lace,
The same old gown, the same old braid,
A new and sweeter face;
The while we whirled in dreamy waltz
My thoughts in fancy flew,
I wondered was the world as false
When that old lace was new

Did hearts as often sigh and break?
Did sorrow walk the land?
Did circumstance make men forsake
The future they had planned?
Were ears by subtle flattery fed?
Were friends, as now, untrue?
Did maids for love, not wealth, then wed,
When that old lace was new?

Or did an honest heart and hand
Above all else suffice
To merit praise, and virtue stand
Pre-eminent o'er vice?
Was fashion's whirl as giddy then?
Did hopes of fame imbue
The hearts and brains of worldly men,
When that old lace was new?

The music ebbs and dies away,
Reflections lose their charm,
A face looks up in winning way,
A hand is on my arm.
Love reigns supreme to-day as then,
We learn by rote to woo,
The same old passion lives in men
As when that lace was new.

Roy Farrell Greene.

THE NIGHT BEFORE HER WEDDI

"I hear you are in for running off with another man's wife. Poor, despised creature!"
"I am not altogether despised, madame. He sends me flowers every day."

HER RIVAL FRIEND

"I said a nasty thing about Miss Catting the other day, but I assure you it was unintentional."
"Well, Jack, seeing it's you, I'll overlook the fact of its being unintentional."

A QUESTION OF QUALITY.

"You will get over it. It was only your puppy love."
"Oh, but he was such a nice puppy!"

AVUNCULUS He was no greater than George Washington.

THE NEW WOMAN: George Washington? He was Martha Washington's husband, wasn't he?

A SUMMER SCENE.

MAIDS, WIVES AND WIDOWS.

THE NEW ADDITION.

"Owing to the recent increase in my family, I have had to take a new house."
"Boy or girl?"
"Son-in-law."

"The second time I saw him I was engaged to him."
"What caused the delay?"

IN CONFIDENCE.

"So those are your husband's ancestors? Aren't they impressive!"

THE AMERICAN COUNTESS: Yes, as a rogues' gallery.

IT LOOKED THAT WAY.

"Your father has an idea that you are going to marry a worthless, good-for-nothing fellow, but aha! I will fool him!"

"Gracious! You are not going to break off the engagement, are you?"

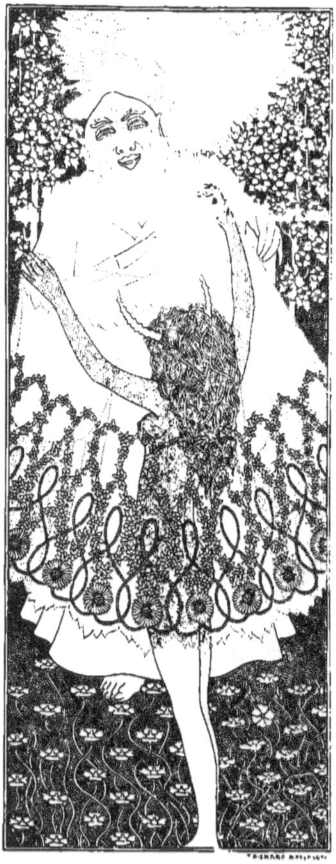

THE TEMPTATION OF ST. ANTHONY

ENCOURAGING HIM.

He: I could kiss the very ground upon which you walk.

"Foolish boy! I'm sure the ground would not appreciate it."

THE BASHFUL ONE: Why do you girls always kiss each other when you meet?
SHE: Because we wish to do unto each other as we would that others should do unto us.

LIFE IN THE METROPOLIS

"Oh, John! No room for a trunk! Why not put it in the air-shaft bedroom?"
"Can't; there's a bandbox there already."

"TO me I swear [illegible]
But she said, with judicial look,
"Your oath's not valid at Common Law
Until you've kissed the Book."

J. H. Thacher.

QUITE VISIBLE.

"Have you any visible means of support?"
"Oi'd loike t' know phat ye call thot!"

NOT HIS FAULT.

"Pardon me, madame, but is one of the persons a man?"

"They are both women."

"Oh, Venus!! Another arrow wasted!"

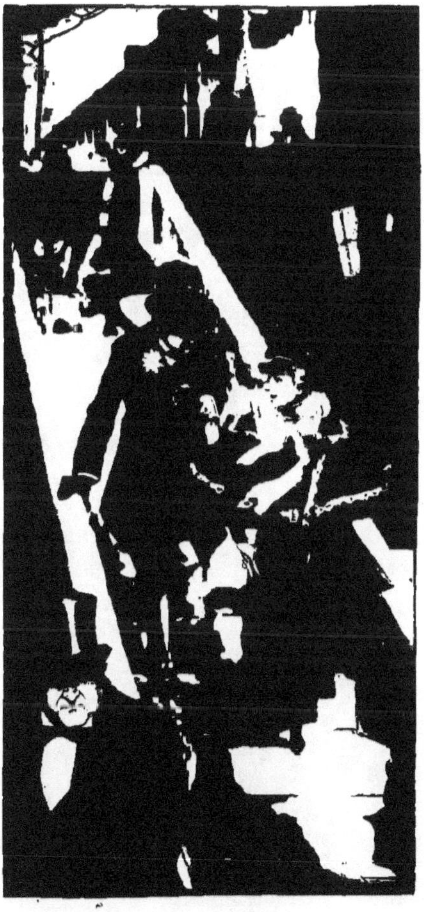

"But papa says you owe everywhere—that you are not a man of honor."
"I assure you, one of the strongest feelings that animate me in entering into this match is the desire to pay my debts."

"THAT DOESN'T APPLY TO ME."

A BRILLIANT WOMAN.

"Tell us how you first discovered your daughter had talents for the operatic stage."
"Well, even in the cradle she was the most quarrelsome child I ever knew."

LIFE'S COMEDY.

LORDS OF CREATION.

AN EXPEDIENT.

"Let's go to the roof garden to-night."

"I don't dare leave the baby, dear."

"Well, I tell you what we'll do. *I'll* go."

RECIPROCITY.

"Pop, I wish you wouldn't smoke when I am around."
"Why not, Willie?"
"Well, I don't when *you* are around."

"I wonder why Mrs. Templeton wears such a wry face?"
"To harmonize with her husband's rye nose."

LORDS OF CREATION.

MR. FOOTISIT: Do you think it rude to ask a lady her age?
"Yes, but not so rude as to try and guess it."

SUITOR: "In my present precarious position, sir, and with my small salary, I don't think there is any possibility of my being able to support your daughter."

"Then what under heavens do you want to marry her for?"

"Because I may lose the position I now hold!"

INEQUALITIES OF CULTURE.

A New York man reading a letter from a Boston girl.

SOMETHING TO BE THANKFUL FOR.

THE DOCTOR: It would be unprofessional in the extreme, Madame, to see the patient until your family physician has been notified.

WIFE: But my husband is dying, Doctor!

"Then, Madame, he will die in the proud consciousness that it is due to the fact that a medical man refused, at a critical time, to commit a breach of professional etiquette."

"He called me a colossal ass!"
"Well, you *are* large."

THE BRITISH SIDE OF IT

"How much does his Lordship get for marrying her?"
"A cool million."
"Worth every cent of it."

THE CAPTAIN (boisterously): Come, old man, brace up! What's got into you?
"If you don't put me ashore you'll very soon see."

"So that's your sister; and I suppose that gentleman in the military uniform is your father."

ALL SHE ASKED

He (at the soirée): May I not offer you some refreshment?
"Yes. Just give me a few minutes to myself."

"Do you know, I'm quite worried about myself. I really believe I am losing my nerve."
"How do you notice it?"
"I'm getting so I hate to ask anyone for a loan. As soon as I saw you I began to tremble."

PATER (angrily). My father never gave me half as much as I allow you.

"Were you satisfied?"

"Of course I was."

"Then why should he?"

HER HOBBY
SHE was a beauty, blithe and blonde,
I met her down at Miss Van Tweedle's,
Her fascinating smile was fond,
Her eye was brighter than a beadle's.
The men who hung about her there —
She called them Billy, Ben and Bobby —
All had a most adoring air;
Collecting hearts—that was her hobby!
Her's was the true collector's skill,
The true collector's keen insistence;
Not long could one against her will,
Howe'er determined, make resistance.
My heart? you ask. Ah, woe is me!
'Tis gone—to my supreme dejection;
For down at Miss Van Tweedle's tea
She added it to her collection!

LORDS

THE ONLY PE

"How did I get in last night, James?"
"On your hands and knees, sir."

SOME ADVANTAGES OF A COLLEGE EDUCATION.

NOT THAT KIND.

"Say, Bill didn't you say that matches were made in heaven?"

"Why, yes."

"Well, yer can't fool me on the smell of that one"

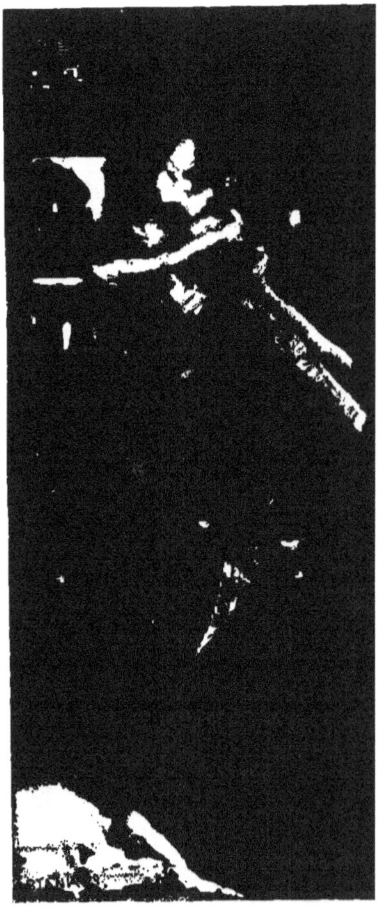

UNRELIABLE.

HE: If you do not accept me, I shall shoot myself.

SHE: But you change your mind so often!

LORDS OF CREATION.

A DIRECT APPEAL.

HE: Do you believe that money has a personality?

SHE: I don't know. Why?

"Here's a telegram I just got from my wife at the seashore, addressed to 'One Hundred Dollars,' in my care."

"What does it say?"

"It says 'Come at once.'"

SHE: What do you want?
"Rest!"
"Well, you better call in at the graveyard, down on the next lot."

"Were the sanitary police in your house this afternoon?"
"They were."
"What was the matter?"
"I was smoking that cigar you gave me."

"I play poker with the old man and make love to his daughter."
"Is it a winning game?"
"Well, I expect soon to hold a hand that will beat his."

ALMOST, BUT NOT QUITE.

"Has your aunt's will been admitted to probate yet?"

"No. There is so much trouble about the pesky thing that I almost wish aunt had never died."

LIFE'S COMEDY

"Bilkins has just returned."

"Where has he been?"

"To Monte Carlo, to win enough to pay his wedding expenses."

"And the wedding?"

"Has been postponed for two years."

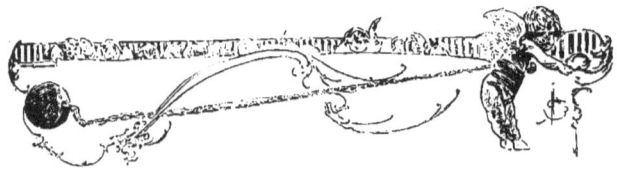

A DESOLATE WORLD.

"Oh, yes, George! You'll get over it and marry some other girl."
"What other girl is there?"

HE: You like the Baron?
"Why, he seems a perfect gentleman."
"Yes, but you know he's traveling *incog.*"

"Dere's two dudes. Bill, let's hold 'em up."
"Oh, de poor t'ings! Dey need de money more dan we do."

SEEING IS BELIEVING

"By Jove, old chap, how I wish there was no such thing as money!"
"Well, we have no positive proof that there is."

LORDS OF CREATION.

MUTUAL.

AMATEUR ACTOR: I am afraid, old man, I shall have to kiss your wife in the third act. You won't mind it, will you?
HIS INTIMATE FRIEND: Not if you don't.

ALL SORTS AND CONDITIONS.

NOTHING BETTER.

"Tell me, Doctor, what do you consider an ideal case?"
"A healthy man with an incurable disease."

ST VALENTINE'S DAY.

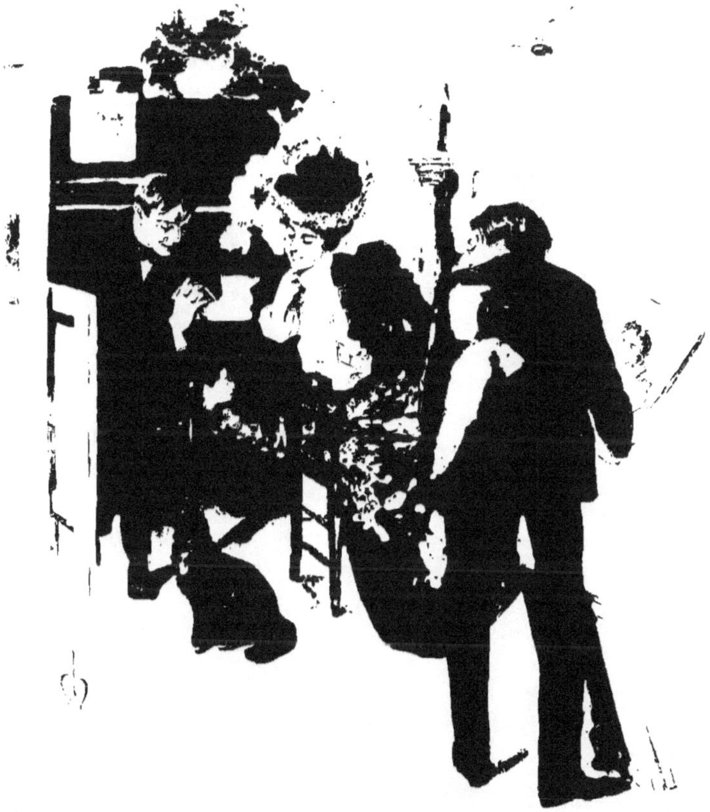

"Well, if that dog hasn't superhuman instinct! He recognizes your portrait of me, Dick."

AT TRINITY

A BURST of airy wings outspread,
  Rosettes (she calls them *choux*),
A bit of lace, a fluff of tulle,
  An artful bud or two
To match the pinky bloom that sweeps
  Across her cheek, and that,
The essence of simplicity,
  Is Peggy's Sunday hat!

When bravely down the aisle it goes
  In time for morning prayer,
What envy pouts upon the lips
  Of every rival fair!
And who can wonder that the chants
  Are sung a trifle flat,
With all the choir looking straight
  At Peggy's Sunday hat?

I, sitting in the pew behind,
  Through sermon, psalm and hymn,
Am baffled by the curve and droop
  Of that provoking brim.
I long to brush my finger-tips,
  In one audacious pat,
Across the rippled hair half-hid
  By Peggy's Sunday hat.

But patience! When the bells ring out
  To set the crowd astir,
And in the porch a flock of lads
  Waits for a smile from her,
For me she has a glance so shy
  My heart grows warm thereat,
And homeward walks my London tile
  With Peggy's Sunday hat.

M. E. W.

PROGRESS IN THE TROPICS.

"Well, what of the captive?"

"Your Majesty, she is a perfect peach!"

"A peach! Then let her be served for dessert with cocoanut cream!"

A FANCY, OR, WINTER AS IT ISN'T.

NOAH: How old are ye?

THE OTHER: Well, I'm six hundred.

"Goodness me! I'm only five hundred and ninety-eight. I ain't a kid myself."

AT THE OPERA

THE Opera Season cannot fail
    To capture rich society,
For those who are not musical
    At least love notoriety;
And box holders are put on show
    Each night with grave formality
(The programmes name them in a row,
    Explaining their locality).

They all belong to the élite,
    Their blood is blue—supposedly;
Though some have known the smell of meat,
    And some sold socks composedly.
Their daughters make a rare display—
    The mothers in complicity—
With costumes cut décolleté,
    Regardless of publicity

The intermission curtain drops—
    A thousand glasses glare at them;
While half as many naughty fops
    Their printed names compare with them
The "gallery god" looks smiling down,
    Informing all the neighbors that
"The fat girl in the ermine gown
    Is Miss De Vere Von Taborstadt.

"That bald-head, seated by the rail,
    Who parts his hair so tastily,
Once languished in the county jail
    For getting rich too hastily.
The red haired girl in salmon pink—
    Her maiden name was Ogleman—
Has been divorced three times, I think,
    And now has hooked a nobleman."

So, while the tongue of scandal wags,
    The exhibition flourishes;
And, as the gossip never flags,
    The interest never perishes
They cannot miss this scrutiny,
    But we will grant, in charity,
There is one thing they fail to see—
    Their manifest vulgarity

His Lordship: "We have a different sense of humour from you Americans. And it's really better, don't you know."
"Yes, he who laughs last laughs best."

SHE WAS JUSTLY PROUD OF HER ANCESTORS.

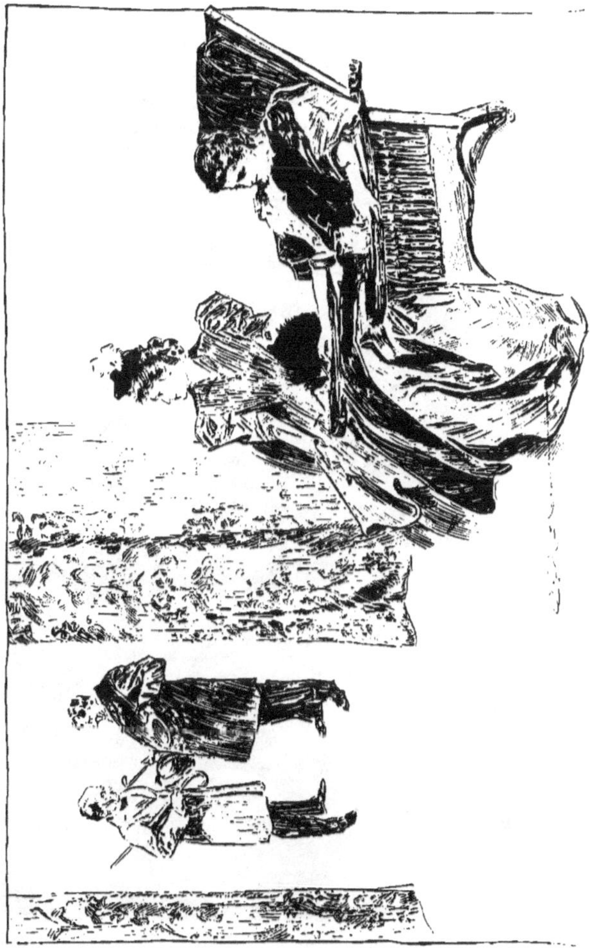

"Don't the doctors agree about your case?"

"No. They haven't had a chance to see each other alone until now."

THERE IS SOMETHING BESIDES MONEY AROUND WALL STREET.

A Little Lesson from Anacreon

I SAT and read Anacreon.
  Moved by the gay, delicious measure,
I learned that lips were made for love
  And love to lighten toil with pleasure.

Just then a laughing girl came by
  With something in her look that caught me;
Forgotten was the poet's song.
  But not the lesson he had taught me.

Charles G. D. Roberts.

ALL FOR A BIRD

ALL SORTS AND CONDITIONS.

FOR TWO.

AN ECONOMIST.

"I say, Dad, why not save time, and bless the food just before it's brought in from the kitchen?"

ALL SORTS AND CONDITIONS.

"His father left several millions and he hasn't brains enough to realize it."
"Poor fellow! What can he do?"
"Well, he's got to choose between Medicine and the United States Senate."

ALL SORTS AND CONDITIONS.

AT THE HIGHER CULTURE SOCIETY.

THE HON. HUMPHREY SLIDER, 5 P.M.: My friends, what we need is to fix our minds on higher things—in our readings, in our conversations, in our entertainments.

THE HON. HUMPHREY SLIDER, 8.40 P.M.: I thought that in such attire, and in such company, I would pass unnoticed; but—shades of Browning! the whole society has fixed its mind on the same idea.

LENTEN VOGUE.

NOW her sins she repents
  Though you'd scarcely expect it!
But a place to commence?
At what charming offense?
'Twould puzzle the sense
  Of a saint to select it!
But her sins she repents—
  Nowadays "they" expect it.

Wood Levette Wilson.

A HOPEFUL PROSPECT.

SHE: Of course, there will never be an American Pope.
THE BROTHER: Why not? Isn't there a Pope Manufacturing Company in this country?

THOSE AMAZING PASTORALS

"I want to put an 'ad' on your drop curtain."
"All right. Shall we have the scene painter do it?"
"No, I'll get a sign painter. I want something pretty good."

"How was he killed, Major?"
"Run over in Brooklyn."
"Oh, those deadly trolley cars!"
"Who said he was run over by a trolley car?"
"Then what ran over him?"
"A baby carriage."

AN ANXIOUS MOMENT

A FORM OF SPEECH.

HE: I ran across grandmother in the Park, yesterday

HIS AUNT: Oh, dear! I didn't know that you rode a bicycle.

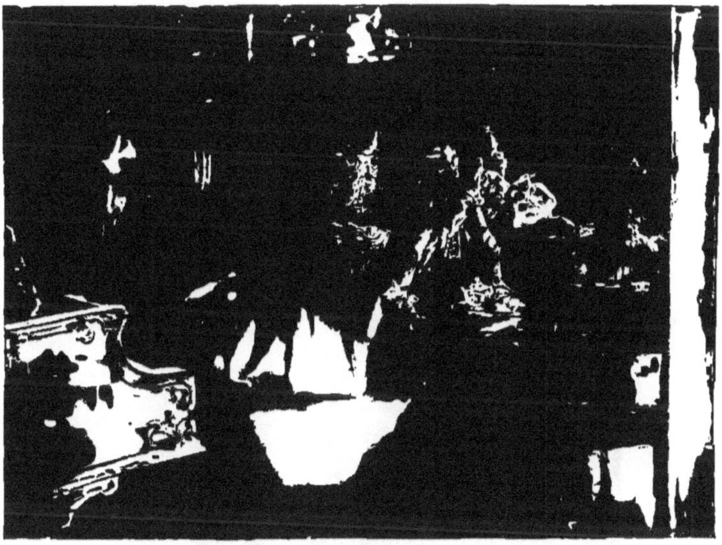

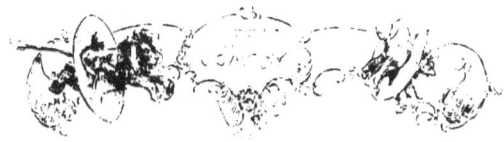

AN AGE OF MIRACLES

THE HOSTESS Society possesses a power that is almost magical

"It does, indeed How easily, for instance, it transforms an ass into a lion"

PROBABILITIES FOR 1947

MR. FATTMASHER: She's looking right at me now.
"Go along—she's only guessing at your weight."

WHEN THE SCOTCH DIALECT REACHES JAPAN.

HIS MOTHER'S BOY.

"Papa, don't say *must* to me; it makes me feel *won't* all over."

AT THE STUDIO DOOR.

www.ingramcontent.com/pod-product-compliance
Lightning Source LLC
Chambersburg PA
CBHW020751020726
47495CB00008B/2384
* 9 7 8 3 3 3 7 1 0 4 0 2 3 *